Special thanks to Linda Chapman

To Charlotte and Holly Allison
- believe in magic!

ORCHARD BOOKS

First published in Great Britain in 2013 by Orchard Books
This edition published in 2017 by The Watts Publishing Group

3 5 7 9 10 8 6 4

© 2013 Hothouse Fiction Limited
Illustrations © Orchard Books 2013

The moral rights of the author and illustrator have been asserted.
All characters and events in this publication, other than those clearly in the public domain,
are fictitious and any resemblance to real persons, living or dead, is purely coincidental.

A CIP catalogue record for this book is available from the British Library.

ISBN 978 1 40834 830 7

Printed in Great Britain by Clays Ltd, Elcograf S.p.A.

The paper and board used in this book are made from wood from responsible sources

Orchard Books
An imprint of Hachette Children's Group
Part of The Watts Publishing Group Limited
Carmelite House, 50 Victoria Embankment, London EC4Y 0DZ

An Hachette UK Company
www.hachette.co.uk
www.hachettechildrens.co.uk

Series created by Hothouse Fiction
www.hothousefiction.com

Dream Dale

ROSIE BANKS

ORCHARD

This is the
Secret Kingdom

Dream Dale

Contents

Bedtime's Boring

Ellie Macdonald was playing catch
in her back garden with her two best
friends, Summer Hammond and Jasmine
Smith. Jasmine had just thrown the ball
high into the air and Ellie and Summer
were both running to catch it when
Ellie's mum opened the back door.

"Girls!" she called.

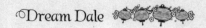

Ellie turned to look, and Summer
crashed into her with a bump. "Oops!"
she giggled as she and
Ellie fell in a heap
on the floor.
"Sorry, are
you okay?"
Ellie
grinned.
"I'm all
right. I fall
over so often
anyway that I'm
used to it!"
Mrs Macdonald smiled. "Whoops,
sorry, girls! I just wanted to ask Ellie if
she'd put Molly to bed for me. I've got
a load of paperwork to catch up on this
evening."

"Sure, Mum!" Ellie said. Molly was her four-year-old sister. Ellie loved being a big sister, even though Molly was a bit naughty at times!

"We'll help," offered Summer.

Mrs Macdonald smiled. "Thanks! There's some popcorn in the kitchen for all of you when you've finished." She disappeared back into the house.

"Yum!" declared Jasmine. "It won't take us long to get Molly into bed and then we can eat the popcorn and watch a DVD."

Ellie and Summer grinned at each other.

"What?" said Jasmine, seeing their expressions. "It can't be *that* hard to put Molly to bed."

"You don't know what little brothers

and sisters are like!" Ellie told her.

"Finn and Connor never go to bed without a fight!" Summer agreed, thinking of her two younger brothers.

"It'll be fine," Jasmine said airily. "After all, if we can beat Queen Malice, I reckon we can do anything!"

The girls grinned at each other. They shared an amazing secret – they could go to a magical world that  no one else knew about! The Secret Kingdom was an enchanted place full of incredible creatures like mermaids,

unicorns, elves and fairies. But the
beautiful land was in great trouble. When
lovely King Merry had been chosen
to rule instead of his sister, evil Queen
Malice, the wicked queen had sworn that
she'd make everyone in the kingdom as
miserable as she was. Summer, Ellie and
Jasmine had managed to stop a lot of
her terrible plans, but now she'd put a
horrible curse on her own brother!

She'd given King Merry a poisoned
cake that was slowly turning him into
a horrible creature called a stink toad.
The only way to cure the king was for
him to drink a counter-potion, but to
make it the girls had to find six very rare
ingredients. They had to get them all and
cure the king before the Summer Ball
or King Merry would be a stink toad

forever! The girls, their pixie friend Trixi, and her aunt Maybelle were the only ones who knew it was happening because the pixies had cast a forgetting spell, so everyone else – including the king himself – forgot about the terrible curse. The girls had promised to do anything they could to secretly help their friend.

"At least we've found two of the ingredients for the counter-potion already," Jasmine said as they went inside to find Molly. "And hopefully we'll be called back to the Secret Kingdom to find another one soon!"

Molly was already in her pyjamas. She looked just like a younger version of Ellie with her dark red curls and dancing green eyes. She had put all the sofa cushions on the floor and was leaping off the sofa onto them. "Hello!" she said, springing up excitedly. "Have you come to play with me?"

"No, we're not going to play with you, you little monkey," said Ellie. "It's bedtime."

"But bedtime's boring! I'll go to bed if you play shops with me first!" Molly bargained. "Pleeeease!" she added, taking Jasmine's hands and looking up at her, her green eyes wide.

"Oh, all right." Jasmine smiled at her. "Just one game."

"Mistake," Ellie whispered to Summer.

Summer giggled.

"You absolutely promise you'll go to bed after one game?" Ellie asked.

"Oh, yes," answered Molly, nodding. "I promise."

It was the longest game ever. Jasmine was lining Molly's teddy bears up for what felt like the hundredth time when Ellie interrupted. "Okay, Molly, it really is bedtime now," she said firmly. "Remember, you promised."

Molly grinned at her. "I promised to go to bed – I didn't promise to go to sleep! Race you upstairs!"

She scampered away.

Jasmine groaned. "Okay, you two were right! This *is* going to go on forever!"

They went upstairs. Molly was jumping on her bed, singing loudly.

"Come on, Molly, into bed now," said Summer, going to the window and drawing the curtains.

"Don't shut them all the way!" Molly protested. "I like looking at the stars.

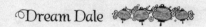

They stop me feeling scared of the dark."
Summer left the curtains open a bit.

"I need another blanket!" Molly
whined to her sister.

"Oh, all right!" Ellie sighed. She headed
to her room and grabbed her blanket off

her bed. As she took it she glanced at her desk. On it was the beautiful magic box that had come from the Secret Kingdom. It was carved with all sorts of magical creatures and studded with beautiful gemstones and there was a mirror on the lid which was...*sparkling and shining*! Ellie's heart did a somersault. It must be another message from Trixi, their pixie friend in the Secret Kingdom!

Snatching up the blanket, she raced back to Molly's room. "Here you are!" she gabbled, throwing it over her sister. "Jasmine! Summer! You've got to come to my room. We'll be back in a minute, Molly!"

She raced to her room with Jasmine and Summer following curiously.

"What's up?" asked Jasmine.

Ellie shut the door behind them.
"Look!" She pointed excitedly at the
Magic Box. Summer and Jasmine gasped
as they saw that words were already
forming in the mirrored lid.

"The Secret Kingdom needs our help again!" exclaimed Ellie in delight.

Trouble in the Secret Kingdom

Summer and Jasmine gathered round as Ellie read out the words glowing in the lid of the Magic Box.

"Dear friends, please help or
I shall weep.
I just can't get the king to sleep!
Please come to where the gold flags fly
From turrets pink, high in the sky."

The three girls looked at each other. "Easy!" they all said.

"It's got to mean King Merry's palace!" Summer smiled. "That has pink turrets!"

"Come on!" Jasmine cried. "Let's go!"

They put their hands on the green gems that studded the glowing box and chorused, "The answer to the riddle is the Enchanted Palace!"

The Magic Box glowed even more brightly and suddenly there was a flash of silver light. A tiny pixie sitting on a floating leaf had appeared on the desk, landing next to a shell that Ellie had been drawing the day before. She was wearing a long pale-pink nightdress that reached down to her toes. Her messy blonde hair was loose under a petal hat.

"Oh!" She smiled as she looked round.
Her face lit up. "Ellie!" She beamed. "And
Summer and Jasmine," she cried, spotting
the other girls. "Hello, girls! Am I at the
beach?" she asked, looking at the shell
in surprise.

"No!" Ellie
giggled.
"You're in my
bedroom."
"It's lovely
to see you all
again." Trixi
flew her leaf
over to them
and placed
feather-light
kisses on each of
their noses.

"What's going on, Trixi?" Jasmine asked her. "What does the riddle mean?"

"Well…" The little pixie stopped talking as she gave a huge yawn. "Oh dear. Please excuse me. I'm just so tired! I don't know what's going on, but no one in the Secret Kingdom seems to be able to get to sleep. I read King Merry a bedtime story every night and usually he falls asleep straight away, but last night I read all night long and he was still wide awake!"

"You poor thing," Summer said kindly. "Why can't people get to sleep?"

"No one knows," replied Trixi worriedly. "I sent you the message because I was hoping you could come and help work out what was going on."

"Hmm," Jasmine frowned. "It sounds

like Queen Malice's work to me."

Trixi's eyes widened. "Maybe! Oh dear, will you come and help?"

"Of course!" Summer said.

"Oh, thank you!" Trixi gave another yawn.

"If we're in the Secret Kingdom maybe we can look for the next missing ingredient while we're there," Ellie said eagerly. "Has Maybelle worked out what else we need?"

Trixi shook her head. Her aunt Maybelle was a very wise old pixie who was trying to find out what ingredients they needed for the counter-potion to cure King Merry. "She has been working really hard trying to figure out what they are, but I don't think she knows yet." She held up her pixie ring and yawned again. "Are you ready to go?"

"Definitely!" cried the girls.

Trixi tapped her ring and called out a spell.

"Good friends, you come at my request
To help King Merry get some rest."

A stream of silver-and-pink sparkles flew from Trixi's ring. They surrounded the girls in a glittering cloud, whizzing around them faster and faster. Summer grabbed the others' hands as she felt the magic whirlwind lift them up. "Here we go!" she cried.

They spun and tumbled around until they suddenly felt themselves dropping down. "Oof!" gasped Ellie as she sank down into the comfiest, softest bed she

had ever seen. It was about ten times
as big as her parents' bed and was
surrounded by a gorgeous golden canopy,
held up by four golden pillars. Between
the pillars were deep red velvet curtains
that were drawn shut. Summer reached
up to her head and smiled as she felt
the pink hearts of her tiara. Their tiaras
always magically appeared on their

heads when the girls came to the Secret
Kingdom, to show everyone that they
were important guests and helpers of the
king.

"Where are we?" Ellie said, looking at
the bed.

Jasmine pulled back the heavy red
curtains and the girls peeked out.

They were in a massive bedroom. There was gold wallpaper on the walls and the ceiling was covered with a beautiful painting of unicorns, mermaids and fairies. A glittering chandelier hung down decorated with hundreds of tiny, twinkling stars.

"Crowns and sceptres!" cried a surprised voice. "What in the Secret Kingdom is going on?"

"King Merry!" exclaimed Ellie, turning and seeing the tubby, rosy-cheeked king walking towards the bed. He was wearing a purple velvet dressing gown, purple-and-white striped pyjamas and a long white nightcap underneath his royal crown. His half-moon spectacles were perched on the end of his nose, and he was holding a purple teddy bear, which had its own crown on.

"My human friends from the Other Realm!" gasped King Merry. "Goodness gracious me!"

"I brought them here, Your Majesty!" Trixi peeked down over the edge of the golden canopy. "I was hoping they could help us work out why no one can get to sleep."

"What an excellent plan!" beamed King Merry. He opened his arms and the girls all climbed down from the bed and gave him a hug. "It's lovely to see you... *RIBBIT!*"

The king gave a very loud toad-like croak and clapped his hands to his mouth. "Oh, goodness, I do beg your pardon." His rosy cheeks flushed even redder. "I have this very annoying cough at the moment."

"Don't worry at all, King Merry," Jasmine soothed.

King Merry gave a little hop and bounced up onto his bed. Jasmine bit her lip. Oh dear, King Merry was even more toad-like than the last time she'd seen him!

"We have to find the magic ingredients,"

she whispered anxiously to Summer and Ellie.

"What's that, my dear…*RIBBIT!*" said King Merry. He clapped his hands to his mouth again.

"Oh dear, Your Majesty!" Trixi wrung her hands. "I really think you should lie down and try to sleep."

Just then there was a knock on the bedroom door and an older pixie flew in on her floating leaf.

"Aunt Maybelle!" said Trixi.

Trixi's aunt had grey hair swept up in an elegant bun, a long sparkling green dress and very kind eyes. "Oh, hello! I was just coming to see if you wanted me to magic you a warm milky drink to help you sleep, Your Majesty." She flew her leaf over to the king and tapped her pixie ring. A steaming mug appeared next to the bed. "King Merry, you look very tired. Why don't you have a rest while the girls come with me?"

"Oh, lovely!" King Merry stretched as he climbed into bed. "I don't think I'll be able to sleep..." He yawned. "But I'll try!" Pulling the covers up around his chin, he let his nightcap fall over his eyes.

Summer, Jasmine and Ellie followed Trixi and her aunt out into the corridor.

"I'm so glad you are here, girls. I've just found out what the next ingredient we need is!" Aunt Maybelle whispered as Trixi pointed her ring at the door to shut it behind them.

"The next ingredient! What is it?" Ellie asked eagerly.

"Dream dust!" Aunt Maybelle declared.

"But what's that?" asked Summer.

"Dream dust is made by the dream dragons every night," explained Trixi. "They scatter it over the entire kingdom when it gets dark, so everyone falls asleep and has lovely dreams."

"Oh, wow!" Summer felt a rush of excitement. "That sounds amazing. Where do we have to go to get some?"

"The dream dragons live in a gorgeous valley called Dream Dale," Trixi told them.

Ellie was looking thoughtful. "Maybe the reason no one can sleep at the moment has something to do with the dragons! We might be able to solve two problems at once if we go and see them!"

"Then what are we waiting for?" cried Jasmine, grabbing the others' hands. "Let's go and meet the dream dragons!"

Dream Dale

Trixi tapped her pixie ring and chanted:

"To the dale where dragons roam
Take us now to see their home!"

Suddenly a warm wind rushed through
the palace and whisked them away. The
wind carried them across the kingdom
until they reached a wide valley,
surrounded by rocky purple hills. The

lower slopes were covered with cherry
trees blooming with clouds of pink-and-
white flowers that ruffled on the branches
as they passed. A sparkling silver river
wound round green-and-gold weeping
willow trees, and butterflies fluttered
through the air. And underneath the trees
walked nine large dragons, their scales
glittering in the sunlight!

Ellie, Summer and Jasmine landed in
the long thick grass and looked round.
Tiny white butterflies settled on their
hair and shoulders, making Ellie giggle
in delight. But what really made the girls
gasp was the sight of the dream dragons.

"Wow!" breathed Summer. She'd always
wanted to meet a dragon!

The dragons were all different colours.
They looked rather like pictures Summer
had seen of Chinese dragons, with big,
rounded, horse-like heads, large dark
eyes, long tails and four legs with big
clawed feet. They didn't have wings but
their beautiful scales shone. Some of them
were eating the lush grass, and others
were rolling on their backs in the blossom
or nuzzling each other like enormous
pussy cats.

"Look at them all!" breathed Jasmine.

"They're so beautiful!" said Ellie, her
fingers itching to draw them.

"They're very friendly too," Trixi told
them. "But I'm surprised they're awake at
the moment. Dream dragons usually sleep
all day and stay awake at night. Perhaps
they're worried about something."

"Maybe they can't get to sleep at the moment, just like everyone else," suggested Jasmine. She could hardly imagine anyone being upset or worried here. Dream Dale was such a beautiful, calm and peaceful-looking place that if she hadn't been so excited about meeting the dragons, Jasmine would have felt like curling up and falling asleep there and then!

A large purple dragon suddenly noticed them. He heaved himself up and came over, his large eyes curious. The others followed him, their clawed feet making the trees shake as they approached.

Ellie had to remind herself that Trixi had said that they were friendly – they were so big! The smallest, a white-and-silver dragon, was the height of a horse,

and the big purple dragon was taller than
an elephant!

"Greetings." The purple dragon stopped
in front of them.

"Hello, Huang. It's me, Trixi!" said Trixi,

flying her leaf over to his massive head
and floating in front of his nose.

The dragon smiled. "Hello, my favourite
pixie," he said, his voice a deep rumble in
his chest. His eyes fell on the girls' tiaras.
"And these must be the human girls from
the Other Realm."

Trixi nodded. "This is Jasmine, Summer
and Ellie."

Huang smiled at the girls. "I am
delighted to meet you. I have heard
about all your adventures here in the
Secret Kingdom."

"We're trying to stop Queen Malice
again at the moment," said Summer,
stepping forward. She was usually shyer
than Ellie and Jasmine but she couldn't
feel nervous around such beautiful
creatures. "She's done something really

horrible to poor King Merry."

The girls explained about the cursed cake and the dream dragons looked horrified.

"We really need some dream dust to put in the counter-potion," Ellie told them.

"You'll give us some, won't you, Huang?" Trixi asked. "We only need a little bit."

Huang looked round. A few of the other dragons hung their heads and the rest looked anxious. Summer felt a chill of worry run through her as she saw their expressions.

"Is…is something wrong?" Jasmine asked slowly.

Huang heaved such a deep sigh that the pink-and-white blossoms on the cherry trees around them trembled. "I'm afraid so."

A pink-and-cream dragon with beautiful long eyelashes and a gentle expression stepped forward. "We'd give you as much dream dust as you need, but we were not able to make any last night" she rumbled.

"Oh!" Ellie gasped. "Is that why no one in the kingdom has been able to go to sleep?"

The dragons all nodded sadly, and the smallest, the white-and-silver dragon, lay down and

covered his eyes guiltily with his large front paws.

"Don't be sad, Chi!" said Trixi, swooping over on her leaf and stroking his head.

The pink-and-cream dragon's large eyes filled with tears. "We are all sad, Trixi. We are so sorry that people cannot sleep."

"What's happened?" asked Ellie.

"For you to understand that, my friends, you must first know how we make dream dust," Huang answered heavily. "Every night, we dream dragons fly up to the top of Dream Dale."

"But how?" Jasmine interrupted, looking at their long scaled bodies and their furry lion-like manes. "You haven't got wings."

"We do not need wings – we gallop through the sky, flying with magic," Huang told her. "Every night as the darkness falls we each soar up to the top of the dale and place one of our scales in one of the nine magic hollows in the rocks. When we circle over the scales each one turns into a glowing dream stone. We heat the stones with our fiery breath until they turn into dream dust. Then we scatter it over the kingdom to send everyone to sleep. But we cannot do that now because…"

"Because we're scared of the dark!" wailed Chi, the little dragon.

"You're afraid of the dark!" Ellie stared at them. "But why? You're dream dragons!"

"I know," said Chi. "It's never happened

before, but yesterday when night fell it suddenly seemed so terrifying that we just wanted to hide in our caves." He used his tail to point at some caves in the base of the cliffs.

"We went inside and then we couldn't find the courage to come out until it was light," growled Huang. "By then it was too late to make the dream stones and create dream dust."

A low sad moan ran through all the dragons. They all looked so upset that Summer longed to comfort them all! The one next to her bent his head and Summer stroked his velvety ears.

"I bet this *is* something to do with Queen Malice, just like we thought!" Jasmine said angrily to Ellie and Summer. "Remember how she made the elves at the bakery all turn from nice to mean, and how she confused Clara Columbus so that she forgot she was an explorer? This is just the sort of thing she would do!"

"Has Queen Malice been here?" Ellie asked the dragons quickly.

"No," rumbled Huang. "No one has been here for several moons."

"Apart from that nice old lady who came to visit us a few days ago," piped up Chi. "Do you remember? She brought us a basket of delicious lotus-blossom cookies. We all ate one!"

"An old lady brought you cookies?" Jasmine echoed.

"I bet it was Queen Malice in disguise!" groaned Ellie.

Summer bit her lip. "She disguised

herself to get into King Merry's party," she told the dragons. "It sounds like those cookies you ate were enchanted, just like King Merry's cake!"

The dragons looked at each other in dismay. "What are we going to do?" said Chi.

The pink-and-cream dragon looked hopefully at Trixi. "Could you lift the spell and stop us being scared?"

"Oh, I wish I could, Pan!" Trixi said. "But Queen Malice's spells are too strong for my magic to break."

"Does this mean we'll be afraid of the dark forever?" asked Chi shakily.

"And no one in the kingdom will ever get to sleep ever again?" rumbled Pan, tears welling in her beautiful eyes again.

"No!" Summer declared. "Because we'll break the spell."

"But how will you do that?" asked Huang.

Summer looked at Ellie and Jasmine. "I don't know yet. But we'll just have to find a way!" she said determinedly.

Flying High

The girls and Trixi racked their brains
trying to think of some way of breaking
Queen Malice's spell. While they thought,
the gentle dragons fetched them some
pale lychee juice to drink and ripe purple
star-shaped fruit to eat. It tasted like the
most delicious mix of the sweetest plums
and peaches. The girls sat on soft piles of
cherry blossom and ate and drank and

talked to the dragons, but no one came up with any ideas about how to break Queen Malice's spell.

Gradually it started to get dark. Chi padded round hanging up lots of orange lanterns on the branches of the cherry-blossom trees. They were made of paper and looked a bit like tiny glowing suns. There were lots of them and they cast a cheerful glow around the dale, but it didn't seem to reassure the dragons very much. The large creatures clustered together in the light of the lanterns, eyeing the dark shadows around them with big scared eyes.

"I think we'll go into our caves until it gets light," growled Huang. "You are more than welcome to join us."

"But Huang, what about everyone in

the kingdom?" said Ellie in dismay. "No
one will be able to get to sleep again.
Please can't you try and fly up to make
your dream stones?"

"Oh, yes, *please* do," begged Summer, stroking the scales on his neck. "I'm sure you're brave enough!"

"Maybe…" Huang glanced up at the cloudy night sky but then shook his head, his whole body seeming to sag. "I'm sorry. It is just too dark up there. We cannot."

Jasmine rubbed her forehead. There had to be *something* they could do to help. "If only you could take the light with you," she sighed. Her eyes fell on the lanterns. "Hang on," she said as an idea came into her head. "But you *can* do that! Of course! You can take the lanterns into the sky with you! Then it won't be so dark and maybe you won't feel so scared."

"But how would we hold them?" Pan pointed out. "We need our feet to claw the air, and our mouths to breathe on the dream stones."

Jasmine frowned. She hadn't thought of that. "Um…"

"I know!" gasped Ellie. "What about if we rode on your backs and held the lanterns for you?"

Huang frowned thoughtfully. "Well, I suppose that might be possible." Some of the other dragons nodded, others looked unsure.

Summer turned to Ellie. "But wouldn't you be scared up there, flying on the back of a dragon? You hate heights."

Ellie gulped. "I'd do it for King Merry and the Secret Kingdom!" she declared.

"Well…" Pan stepped forward, her claws digging into the soft earth. "If you can be brave then so can I. Ellie, will you do

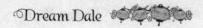

me the honour of riding on my back and
holding the lantern for me?"

Ellie smiled boldly. "Of course." She
unhooked a lantern from a nearby
cherry-blossom tree and walked over
to Pan. The pink-and-cream dragon
crouched down and Ellie scrambled up
onto her back, sitting just behind her

neck with the lantern held high above on
a stick. It cast a bright glow over Pan's
gorgeous scales.

The dragon gave a rumbling growl.
"Brothers and sisters, who will join me
in collecting the dream stones?" she
demanded.

"I will," Huang rumbled. "Jasmine,
would you like to ride on my back?"

"Oh, yes, please!" cried Jasmine in
delight.

"And I will go too!" cried Chi.
"Summer, will you come with me?"

"Yes – definitely!" Summer
exclaimed.

"And I'll fly beside you," declared Trixi,
as Summer and Jasmine took a lantern
each and climbed onto their dragons'
backs. "I'll use my magic to help light up

the way!" She tapped her ring and said in her tinkly voice:

"Magic, make me glow so bright
Like a beacon in the night!"

Instantly Trixi lit up as if she was a glowing firefly! She darted around their heads on her leaf, a spark of white light in the inky-black night.

The dragons padded forwards and, with a great roar, raced between the cherry-blossom trees. Their magic lifted them up into the sky so smoothly that Ellie didn't even notice when Pan's paws left the ground. The dragons' bodies rippled like snakes' through the air as they soared upwards. Summer hung onto Chi's neck, holding the lantern up high as the wind

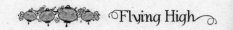

rushed past their faces, sweeping through
their hair.

"Whee!" Jasmine exclaimed as Huang raced past Chi with a playful rumble.

Summer looked round at Ellie. Her face was pale and she was hanging onto Pan's mane tightly. But she was still holding the lantern up to light the way. Summer recognised the determined look in her friend's green eyes. Ellie might be scared, but she wasn't going to let that stop her from helping Pan make a dream stone!

The dragons flew up to the hilltops. When the dale was spread out beneath them, each dragon plucked one of the glittering scales from their chests with their front feet. They each placed a scale in one of the hollows in the rocks. Then they circled in the sky above. Summer caught her breath as she saw Chi's scale glow. It was so bright that she had to look away for a second, and when she turned back the scale had transformed into a smooth, shiny teardrop-shaped stone. Chi's dream stone glowed white, Huang's glistened purple and Pan's shone pink.

"Hooray!" cried Trixi as each of the dragons dived down and scooped up their own dream stone with their front feet. "Now we can fly back down and you can make some dream dust!"

"Race you!" called Jasmine. She leaned forwards and Huang plunged downwards.

But just as she and Chi dived after them, Summer heard a strange flapping noise behind her. She looked over her shoulder and cried out in shock as she saw five dark shapes with leathery bat-like wings racing towards them,

right on Chi's tail! Their horrible beady
eyes glittered against the cloudy sky and
they cackled as they flew.

"Storm Sprites!" Summer yelled.
"Queen Malice's Storm Sprites are
coming to get us!"

A Narrow Escape

Chi galloped faster through the air but the Storm Sprites chased after him, getting closer and closer. Summer realised that the sprites were all holding things that looked like big fat water balloons in their pointy fingers. *Misery drops*, she thought in alarm, remembering another time when the sprites had attacked everyone with them. If the drops touched you, you became too sad to fight back! "Go away!" she yelled at them.

"No!" shrieked the sprites. "We're going

to put out your lanterns and take the
dream stones for Queen Malice!"

Chi snorted in alarm as the leading
sprite darted straight at the lantern
Summer was holding!

"Faster, Chi!" Summer cried, but it was
too late. The sprite threw his misery drop
at the lantern. There was a fizz and a
splutter and the light
suddenly went out!
Summer and Chi
were plunged
into darkness.

"Summer!"
Ellie and Jasmine
shrieked from in front of her.
Summer could just see their worried faces
in the light from their lanterns as they
searched for her and Chi in the darkness.

"It's dark!" Chi roared, swooping round
in a wild panic. Summer let the lantern
go and clung on with her hands and
knees as Chi swerved and veered through
the sky. In his fright he roared again
and dropped the dream stone, which
plummeted to the ground.

Summer was terrified but she knew she had to calm Chi down. It was like reassuring any frightened animal – she had to be the strong one. "It's okay," she soothed, stroking his neck, trying to sound calm. "Please, Chi, please don't be frightened. I'm here with you – you're not alone. We're going to get down safely, I promise."

The dragon slowed slightly. "I'm so scared!"

"Please, don't be," Summer said, sounding calmer than she felt. "I'm here with you."

A dot of light flew towards them. As it got closer Summer recognised the tiny glowing shape. "Trixi!" gasped Summer.

"I've come to give you some light!" cried Trixi as she fluttered by Chi's nose

on her leaf. "The Storm Sprites can't put
me out!"

With Trixi's light and Summer's
soothing words,
Chi stopped
panicking.
Summer
glanced
ahead and
sighed
with relief
as she
saw that
Jasmine and
Ellie's lanterns were
still bobbing through the velvet
night. But then she saw something that
made her heart flip in horror. Ellie
and Pan and Jasmine and Huang had

turned round to come back and help her, and now the Storm Sprites were flying towards them, flapping their leathery wings and cackling nastily.

"Fly away!" Summer yelled at them. "Or they'll put your lanterns out too!"

Realising that Summer was okay, Ellie and Jasmine tried to turn back, but Pan and Huang weren't fast enough. The sprites zoomed closer to the lanterns, lifting up their misery drops…

"We've got to do something!" Summer gasped.

"But what?" said Trixi in despair. "I can't light the way for all three dragons, and if their lanterns go out Huang and Pan will be terrified. Oh, Summer! If only we could break Queen Malice's spell and stop them being scared of the dark!"

Summer looked at the little pixie sparkling by Chi's cheek like a tiny star... Suddenly she remembered what Ellie's sister Molly had said: "*I like to look at the stars when I'm in bed. They stop me feeling scared of the dark.*"

"If only it wasn't so cloudy tonight," she groaned. "Maybe if Huang and Pan could see the light of the stars and moon they wouldn't feel so scared." Suddenly she realised what she had just said. "That's it!" she gasped. "Trixi, can you magic the clouds away?"

"I'll try." Trixi nodded, bouncing up and down on her leaf like a spark in the sky. She tapped her pixie ring and chanted:

"*Dragons do not fear the night
If moon and stars all show their light!*"

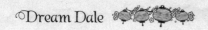

Summer looked around, but the night was just as dark and cloudy as it was before.

"Why didn't it work?" she said desperately.

"I don't know!" Trixi cried. "The only time my pixie magic doesn't work is when I try to use it against Queen Malice's spells."

"Why would Queen Malice want to make it cloudy?" Summer asked. Then suddenly she knew the answer. "Of course! She wanted to stop the dream dragons seeing the stars and breaking her fear spell!"

"That must be it," agreed Trixi. "But what can we do?"

Summer thought as hard as she could. "Would the weather crystal work?" she asked Trixi, thinking of the gift the weather imps had given them. It could control the weather.

Trixi shook her tiny head. "No, I don't think its magic is strong enough."

"Oh, I *wish* there was some way of getting rid of the clouds!" Summer cried desperately, burying her face in Chi's mane. *That was it!* In the Magic Box there was something that could make that wish come true!

"Trixi," she gasped. "Can you summon the Magic Box? We can use one of the three wishes from the glitter dust we collected at Glitter Beach!"

"Good idea, Summer!" Trixi smiled. The little pixie cast a spell and tapped her ring, and with a flash of sparkles the Magic Box appeared in front of her on Chi's back. The effort of summoning it was too much for the tired pixie. She floated down onto Chi's neck, exhausted.

"Just rest, Trixi," Summer said anxiously as she took the tiny bag of glitter dust out of the Magic Box. There was no time to lose! The Storm Sprites were only seconds away from Ellie and Pan.

Just as Summer took a pinch of dust out

of the little silver bag, the Storm Sprites threw their misery drops. They hit Ellie and Jasmine's lanterns and immediately their lights went out. The girls heard the sprites cackling in delight, celebrating as they raced towards the ground. Pan and Huang roared in fright, and Ellie and Jasmine shrieked as they were flung around.

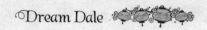

Summer threw the dust into the air and chanted:

"I wish the starry night was clear,
So the dream dragons feel no fear!"

There was a silver flash. Instantly the clouds started to part, and as they did so, Summer saw the clear night sky behind them, with thousands of stars twinkling brightly and a big beautiful full moon.

Chi gasped. "Look at the moon and all the stars! It's not dark at all!"

"How do you feel?" Summer asked anxiously.

"I'm not frightened any more!" Chi roared happily, looping though the air.

"Neither am I!" came a nearby voice.

"Or I!"

In the light of the stars Summer could just make out Jasmine and Huang, and Ellie and Pan, both the dragons' eyes

shining with wonder as they saw the bright stars and the huge full moon which hung like a glowing ball in the dark night sky.

Summer heaved a sigh of relief. Queen

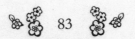

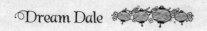

Malice's spell was broken!

"I don't know why I was ever frightened," rumbled Huang as he glanced around.

Pan nodded, her pink-and-cream scales glittering. "It's beautiful up here!"

Summer explained what had happened, and Jasmine and Ellie fussed over Trixi and praised Summer so much that she blushed bright pink. "Phew!" Jasmine sighed. "Well done, Summer! The spell is broken and the Storm Sprites are gone!"

"But we need to get the dream dust more than ever – poor Trixi really needs some sleep!" Summer told the others.

"Let's go and get the dream stones," Jasmine agreed. "Where are they?"

"Oh no!" Pan growled. "I dropped mine when I was frightened."

"But the Storm Sprites are down there!" Ellie cried.

"Queen Malice has been trying to get her hands on our dream stones for ages!" rumbled Chi in dismay. "She wants to give people nightmares!"

"We mustn't let the Storm Sprites get the stones!" Huang roared. "Quick! After them!"

Making the Dream Dust

The three dragons soared down towards the ground. Ellie shrieked and clung on tightly as the wind blew through her hair. She closed her eyes tight and thought about stopping the Storm Sprites.

Powerful Huang raced on ahead of the other two dragons, with Jasmine urging him to go faster. She scanned the ground beneath them as they flew, looking for

any sign of the dream stones. "There!"
she shouted as she spotted one shining
down below. Huang flew faster and faster
as two Storm Sprites flapped out of the
darkness and headed towards it at the
same time. "Stop them, Huang!" cried
Jasmine.

Opening his mouth, Huang gave a
terrifying roar that shook the trees and
bushes in the dale.

The terrified Storm Sprites stopped sharply. "Argh!" one shouted. "I thought dream dragons were supposed to be friendly!"

"You can make friends with him if you want, but I'm off!" yelled the other one.

"Me too!" the first one squealed.

Yelling and shouting, they abandoned the stone and flapped away. Huang dived down and grabbed the precious rock with his front feet.

At the same time, Pan spotted the second dream stone. "I can see it, Ellie!" she called.

Ellie dared to half open her eyes. They were racing down towards the top of a cherry-blossom tree. The dream stone had caught in its branches and a Storm Sprite was already reaching out for it.

There was no way that Pan could get to it first! Ellie's heart sank, but Pan had an idea. Breathing in so deeply that Ellie was shaken up and down on her back, Pan opened her mouth and sent a stream of scorching fire straight at the Storm Sprite. It hit him right on the bottom as his pointy fingers reached out to grab the stone. "Yow!" he screeched, forgetting about the stone as he jumped up and down holding his bottom. "Ow! Oo! Ow!"

"How dare you try and take our dream stones!" Pan roared, sending another fiery breath at the sprite. He dodged it and flew away as fast as his wings would carry him.

Jasmine whooped and cheered from Huang's back. Then she turned to see where Summer and Chi were. They'd disappeared! Jasmine frowned. Where could they have gone? Chi might be the smallest dragon but he was still too big to have vanished completely from sight.

Jasmine scoured the dale below them. "Huang!" she gasped, suddenly spying the final dream stone glittering in the starlight by the edge of the river, next to several large golden weeping willows. "I can see the third stone!"

But they weren't the only ones who

had seen it. The last Storm Sprite was racing towards it. Pan and Huang charged after him. "You can't stop me!" he shrieked as he swooped down to grab it. "I'm going to take this dream stone back to Queen Malice!"

"Oh no, you're not!" Chi roared as he burst out of the willows with Summer and Trixi hanging on tightly to his mane. "BOO!"

The sprite almost jumped out of his skin. "Help!" he shrieked. The three dragons all raced straight at him. The Storm Sprite gave up and dropped the stone on the grass. "Queen Malice can get a dream stone for herself!" he yelped as he fled.

"Hooray!" Summer cheered as Chi swooped down and picked up the dream

stone. Pan and Huang landed on the
ground next to him and Ellie, Summer
and Jasmine looked round. It was
suddenly very quiet. Overhead the stars
were twinkling brightly. The dream stones
had been saved!

"Phew!" Ellie said with a trembling
sigh. She slipped off Pan's back.

The gentle dragon nuzzled her shoulder
with the side of her large rounded head.
"You were very brave."

"I'm just glad the sprites didn't get the dream stones." Ellie looked round at the three dragons. "And you've stopped being scared of the dark! How are you feeling, Trixi?" she added, looking at the little pixie who was resting on Chi's back.

"I'm okay." Trixi gave a brave smile and a huge yawn.

Huang looked happily at the beautiful rocks at their feet. "We have the dream stones back."

"And now we can make dream dust!" said Chi.

"Can we watch you?" Jasmine asked eagerly.

"Of course!" rumbled Pan.

Summer and Jasmine got down and watched with Ellie as the three dragons pushed the stones into a pile and then looked at each other. "Are you ready?" said Huang. "One, two...THREE!"

On the final word, all three dragons breathed out golden fire. It hit the dream stones, which glowed gold, then orange, then red and finally blazed with a white light so bright that it made the girls shut their eyes. They blinked and saw that the flames had vanished. All that was left of the three stones was a pile of white dust that sparkled like the starlight.

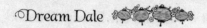

"Dream dust!" the dragons declared.

"Oh, wow!" breathed Ellie. "So now you can make people go to sleep?"

"And have lovely dreams," said Huang, nodding. "Now we can scatter it across the land so that finally all the good people and creatures of the Secret

Kingdom can get some rest. But first..."
He smiled at them and bowed his head
low. "Please take as much as you need
to help dear King Merry. After all, if it
wasn't for you, we wouldn't have any at
all."

"We only need a tiny bit," said Trixi.
She conjured a little golden bag with a
tap of her ring.

Summer, Jasmine and Ellie watched happily as the pixie scooped up some sparkling dream dust into her bag. She put the bag back into her pocket.

"Thank you so much," Summer said to the dragons.

Pan smiled at them all. "Thank *you* for helping us break Queen Malice's spell."

"Now you'll be able to make dream stones and scatter dream dust every night just like you used to," Ellie said happily.

Pan touched her lightly with her nose. "Queen Malice will never be able to make us frightened again. We'll always remember that, although the sky might be covered with clouds, the stars have not disappeared. They are always there, shining brightly even if we cannot see them." She looked up at the glittering sky.

The girls exchanged delighted looks.

"We must gather our brothers and sisters and fly across the land with the dream dust," said Huang.

"We should take this to the palace, so

we can add it to the counter-potion."
Trixi told him.

"We'll be going past the palace. We fly
over every inch of the kingdom scattering
dream dust as we go. Would you do us

the honour of letting us give you a ride there?" said Huang.

"Oh, yes please!" cried Summer and Jasmine.

Ellie hesitated. "Okay!" She gave in with a smile. "But I might keep my eyes shut!"

The Sleeping Kingdom

Huang padded over to the cave where the other dragons were all curled up together, and gave a deep growl. The other dragons came out warily, but as soon as they looked at the twinkling stars their fear faded and they all flew up to make their dream stones. The girls watched as the dream dragons circled overhead, moonlight glinting off their scales. Once they had made their dream dust, all nine dream dragons galloped up into the sky, the girls riding on Pan, Huang and Chi's backs.

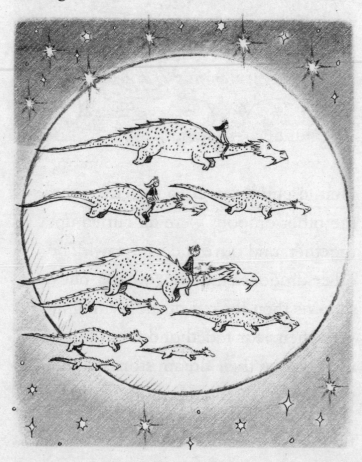

It was the most incredible journey. They swooped across the Secret Kingdom through the twinkling sky, the wind streaming through their hair, with Trixi flying on her leaf beside Ellie. Huang, Pan and Chi had given their dream dust to the girls to scatter. As they passed over Unicorn Valley, Summer gently threw a handful of dust down. As it settled on the grazing unicorns they all stretched and lay down in the lush grass, folding up their legs and resting their muzzles on the ground.

The dragons swooped on past the golden sands and busy, brightly-lit bay of Glitter Beach, where the fairies were wandering around the tiny little stalls and shops on the harbour. As Jasmine scattered her dust the fairies all started to look very sleepy. The fairy children fell asleep on their feet and were scooped up by their parents and carried inside the houses. Soon the streets were deserted as every fairy climbed happily into bed.

Even Ellie joined in. She scattered her dust over the friendly bubblebees that were buzzing around the top of Bubble

Volcano. Moving together, the bees turned and streamed straight into their shining golden hive. Ellie was sure she even saw some of them yawn!

Finally, Huang, Pan and Chi left the other six dragons to swoop over the rest of the kingdom while they carried Trixi and the girls back to King Merry's Enchanted Palace. The dragons hovered next to the coral-pink turrets of the highest tower so that Jasmine, Summer and Ellie could carefully climb off onto the balcony outside King Merry's bedroom. Trixi sleepily flew her leaf up to the windowsill. Inside the tower, the girls could see King Merry pacing up and down next to his huge bed.

"Oh, poor King Merry!" cried Summer in concern. "He looks so tired."

Huang smiled. "Then let us send him to sleep. Girls, are you ready?"

"Yes!" they all cried.

"Then bring sweet dreams to those below," Huang said.

Jasmine, Summer and Ellie threw the last of the dream dust all over the palace. Gradually, just like at Glitter Beach, the lights in the palace were turned out one by one. The girls watched as King Merry climbed into bed, gave one massive yawn and finally fell fast asleep with a big smile on his face.

"He's forgotten to turn his light off!" Trixi stretched her tiny arms above her head. "I'll give this dream dust to Aunt Maybelle and then I'd better go and do that for him. And then I can go to sleep as well!" She smiled sleepily as she

held up the little pouch. "Thank you so much, girls. You didn't just help King Merry get to sleep, you found another ingredient too!"

"We couldn't have done it without the wonderful dream dragons!" said Summer, reaching out to hug Chi. "Thank you!"

The dragons smiled happily.

"It's been an amazing adventure!" sighed Jasmine.

"But now it's time for you to go home." Trixi flew over to the girls on her leaf and kissed each of them on the nose. "I'll see you soon, I hope!"

"Bye, Trixi!" Summer, Jasmine and Ellie cried. "Goodbye, Pan! Goodbye, Huang! Goodbye, Chi!"

"Hopefully we'll see you again soon," Summer added.

Trixi tapped her ring and a glittering cloud of silver sparkles surrounded the girls. It whirled around them, whisking them up and away from the Secret Kingdom, then setting them down gently in Ellie's bedroom.

"Whoa!" said Ellie. Her bedroom suddenly seemed very ordinary. It was hard to believe that just a little while ago they had been swooping through the sky on the backs of dream dragons. "It feels like a dream," she said to the others.

"A very good one!" smiled Summer.

"The best ever!" said Jasmine.

There was the sound of feet running along the corridor and Ellie's door opened. Molly looked in. "What are you doing?" she said naughtily.

"You should be asleep," said Ellie, relieved that no time ever passed in the real world while they were away in the Secret Kingdom. "Come on, Mols, back to bed." She took her sister's hand and led her back to her bedroom.

Jasmine nudged Summer as they

followed. "It's a pity we haven't got any
dream dust to send Molly to sleep."

Summer nodded. "Actually, I think
I have an idea for something else that
might work."

As Ellie tucked Molly into bed, Summer sat down beside her. "You know what often helps my brothers Finn and Connor get to sleep, Molly?"

"What?" Molly asked curiously.

"I tell them a bedtime story," said Summer. "Would you like to hear the story of the dream dragons?"

"Yes, please!" breathed Molly.

Jasmine and Ellie sat down beside Summer on the bed. Summer smiled at Molly. "Once upon a time," she began softly, "in a secret kingdom far away…"

In the next Secret Kingdom
adventure, Ellie, Summer and
Jasmine visit

Lily Pad Lake

Read on for a sneak peek...

Honeyvale
Swimming Pool

"Watch this!" Jasmine called to her best
friends, Ellie and Summer, as she stood
on the side of Honeyvale Swimming
Pool. She dived perfectly into the deep
water, making barely a ripple in the
smooth blue surface.

"Oh, I wish I was brave enough to dive
like that," Summer sighed.

"That was brilliant, Jasmine!" Ellie clapped as Jasmine bobbed up with her long dark hair clinging to her back and a big grin on her face. "My turn now."

Jasmine swam over to watch with Summer as Ellie got out of the pool. Jasmine's grandma waved and smiled at them from the café.

"Geronimo!" Ellie cried, jumping into the air in a star shape and pulling a funny face before plunging down into the water in a tangle of arms and legs.

Summer and Jasmine giggled as droplets of water splashed them.

Ellie surfaced next to them, her green eyes dancing and her usually curly red hair plastered against her head. "At least I didn't do a belly flop," she giggled.

"You try now, Summer," said Jasmine.

"Um…" Summer hesitated. "I don't really like diving and jumping in. The water always gets up my nose."

"Go on, Summer," Ellie urged her. "It's really fun."

Butterflies fluttered in Summer's stomach at the thought and she shook her head.

"It's all right, you don't have to," Jasmine said, seeing her anxious face. "Let's all play chase instead."

"Can we play in the shallow end?" Summer asked hopefully.

Jasmine nodded. "Of course."

"I'm not it!" cried Ellie, speeding off through the water.

"I will be,' said Jasmine. "I'll count to ten. One, two, three…"

Summer splashed away, but even with a head start it didn't take Jasmine long to tag her.

"Got you," Jasmine gasped, touching her arm.

"You're too fast!" Summer laughed.

"Okay, I'll get Ellie instead," Jasmine set off.

Summer smiled as she watched Jasmine chase Ellie across the pool, and dabbled her fingers in the rippling water. She liked swimming but she wished she didn't feel so worried about going out of her depth.

It was so much easier when we were swimming with the mermaids in the Secret Kingdom, she thought to herself. Then she'd been sprinkled with magical bubble dust that had let her breathe underwater.

The Secret Kingdom was a wonderful land that only she, Ellie and Jasmine knew about, where amazing creatures like unicorns, elves and pixies lived. Summer, Ellie and Jasmine had first discovered it when they had found a magic box at their school jumble sale, and since then they'd had all sorts of adventures there. Their pixie friend Trixibelle sent them a message in the Magic Box whenever the Secret Kingdom needed their help.

Summer knew there was trouble in the enchanted land at the moment. King Merry, the happy king, had been given a cursed cake by his sister, evil Queen Malice. She wanted to become the ruler of the land and so she had poisoned the cake with a curse that was slowly turning

King Merry into a horrible creature called a stink toad. If King Merry didn't drink a counter-potion by the time of the Secret Kingdom's Summer Ball he would be a stink toad for good! Summer, Ellie and Jasmine had promised to help find the ingredients to make the counter-potion. So far they had managed to collect bubblebee honeycomb, silverspun sugar and dream dust, but there were still three more ingredients to find, and time was running out.

Summer glanced towards the changing rooms. She and her friends had started taking the Magic Box everywhere with them so that they wouldn't miss a message from the Secret Kingdom. They had left it in Jasmine's bag in their locker while they were swimming. What if their friends in the Secret Kingdom needed them right now? *I'll just go and check it*, Summer thought, pulling herself out of the pool.

The others swam over as they saw their friend get out. "Are you OK, Summer?" Ellie asked.

"Yes," Summer replied. "I'm just going to our locker to have a quick look."

Ellie and Jasmine smiled. They didn't need her to say any more, they knew *exactly* what she meant.

"We'll come with you," Jasmine grinned.

The three of them hurried to the changing room, dripping water as they went.

When they reached their locker they stopped. A light was shining out around the edges of the locker door!

"The Magic Box!" gasped Jasmine. "It's glowing!"

Ellie checked around. Luckily there was no one else in the changing room to see. "Quick. Let's get it out and see if it has a riddle for us!"

Read
Lily Pad Lake

to find out what happens next!

Be in on the secret.
Collect them all!

Series 1

When Jasmine, Summer and Ellie discover
the magical land of the Secret Kingdom,
a whole world of adventure awaits!

Secret Kingdom

Bubble
Volcano

ROSIE BANKS

Sugarsweet
Bakery

ROSIE BANKS

Dream Dale

ROSIE BANKS

Lily Pad
Lake

ROSIE BANKS

Midnight
Maze

ROSIE BANKS

Fairytale
Forest

ROSIE BANKS

Series 2

Wicked Queen Malice has cast a spell to
turn King Merry into a toad! Can the girls
find six magic ingredients to save him?

Secret Kingdom

Wildflower Wood
ROSIE BANKS

Swan Palace
ROSIE BANKS

Snow Bear Sanctuary
ROSIE BANKS

Phoenix Festival
ROSIE BANKS

Fancy Dress Party
ROSIE BANKS

Jewel Cavern
ROSIE BANKS

Series 3

When Queen Malice releases six fairytale baddies into the Secret Kingdom, it's up to the girls to find them!

Secret Kingdom

Have you read all the books in Series Four?

Meet the magical Animal Keepers of the Secret Kingdom, who spread fun, friendship, kindness and bravery throughout the land!

Secret Kingdom

A magical world of
friendship and fun!

Join the Secret Kingdom Club at

www.secretkingdombooks.com

and enjoy games, sneak peeks and lots more!

You'll find great activities, competitions, stories
and games, plus a special newsletter for
Secret Kingdom friends!